• On Ortbook un LSD •
• SEON OEON •

AN
ARTBOOK
ON LSD

· A SEAN AEON EXPRESSION ·

An Artbook on LSD. Copyright © 2025 by Sean Aeon.
All rights reserved.

ISBN 978-1-959810-30-8

LCCN 2025919775

SECOND EDITION

Editor, Artist, Photographer, Designer:

Sean Aeon

www.aeonaes.com

AEONAES.COM

ART & INSIGHT

o

Thank you to Aché, Jatia, Steve, and Roses
for your unending encouragement during this projects assembly

o

° THE PREFACE °

Each chapter begins with one of twelve hand-painted versions of the original *aeonaes* (ee-on-nis) symbol.

Aeonaes represents a bridge between parallel perspectives, the desolation of opposition, and the clarity of complementary existence.

Meaning, "as above, so below", aeonaes is a term from a transcendent language of scribes—part of *aeonilism* (ee-on-ih-liz-uhm)—included in the lush world of LA on LSD.

The *above* is one half of collapse. The *below* is self without awareness.
The conceptual and mechanical functions existing internally and externally are admired equally.

Chapter excerpts from the full LA on LSD short story series are highlighted along with the visuals, each painting their own picture.

Within the glossary, alongside exclusive concept definitions, calligraphy pieces symbolically represent the explored evolving philosophies.

Rooted in similar *continular* movements as the Enzo circle and others (a single, unidirectional curved line), *aeonilist* (ee-on-ih-list) interpretations speak to the execution of all life, performed in one, fluid motion forward.

Enjoy this intersection of art, imagination, and investigation.

THE GRIM REAPED

CHAPTER ONE

• Page Twelve •

Most of what we considered true was only true some of the time. Balance was a solid example. Only asking for balance signified not knowing what we asked for. Balance only broke even. Did we try losing as much money as we made, or hating as much as we loved? Did we ask for the same quantity of what we wanted, as what we didn't? I doubted Ashlyn wanted to feel fifty percent better and fifty percent the same. Aside from it being pointless, we usually didn't wish for half of someone back either.

If all of something wasn't for us, none of it was.

• Page Thirteen •

It reminded me of playing Broken Telephone in school as a kid, no further along than third grade. How would we have known what a rumor was before then? How would we have learned how exhilarating it was to control a narrative? Peculiar lessons were chosen to teach to children. The parents pushing their kids in the stroller, who were old enough to do jumping-jacks, were no different. The parents who physically fought others in front of their children, were worse.

Adults taught children how to be adults. What about that was confusing? It took me awhile to realize how the parent-child dynamic silently confessed. Kids were students.

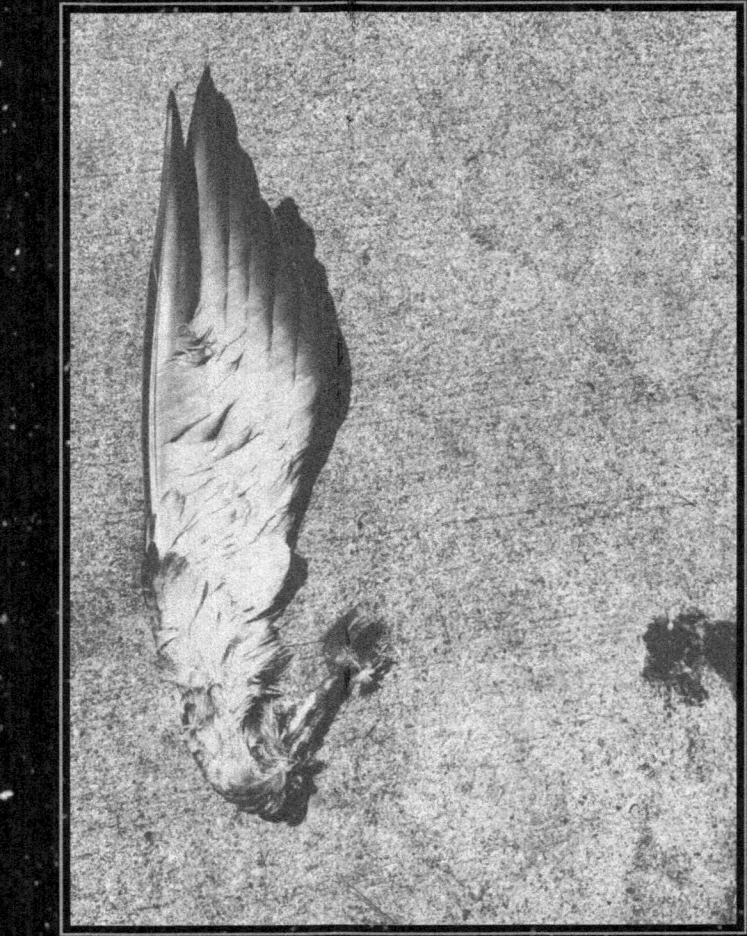

Disorderly children were reflections of parental disorders. God didn't make us, our parents did.

●●●

• Page Eighteen •

Some of us understood villains. Why did we get locked in a cage and consequently find a connection to a higher power? Two reasons. Humanity was on an eternal quest for freedom. Some required the removal of physical freedom in order to free their minds. The removal of one freedom only motivated us to find another. The second reason. The light was not understood before the darkness. Light was brought into existence. Every version and level of wisdom, captured and shared the same view sensibly. We were all at home in the darkness. We were all at peace in the light. The light and dark were options, with differing outcomes for

ourselves and those we encountered. That man walked through the valley of the shadow of death. Most looked inside, turned around at the entrance, then spoke of their intimate exchange with the shadows. Nothing was gained when afraid of loss.

A snake keeping its skin from shedding, only weighed itself down.

●●●

• Page Twenty-One •

Some asked for answers and received obstacles.

Others could only offer us obstacles if we struggled the same. If only we were taught that misdirection was worse than having none.

When standing at the edge of a cliff, it was better to stand still than move forward aimlessly.

•••

• Page Twenty-Two •

Gold didn't shine in the dark.

My friend wasn't lost, he was
misled without understanding.
We all visited that place, but
some became locals. Losing
something wasn't the same as
having it hidden from us. The
weight of California gold,
weighed many to the bottom
of the California coastline.

The city was screaming
to have its story retold so
the narrative could
change, but too much
cash was being made to
hear anything over the
money-counters.

People were killing themselves
for others, living like they
didn't want to be alive.

•••

• Page Twenty-Three •

Love live Landslide.**

** "Love live" is used instead
of "Long live", demonstrating
a life loved; a celebration of
those moving-on to continue
living in their next form.

What good is living long,
without living with love?

••••••

THE UNREVEALED SEEN

CHAPTER TWO

• Page Twenty-Seven •

As I picked up the first pen I saw waiting around with nothing better to do, I thought about writing something. However, unlike the old cliché, I wasn't much of an articulate creative under the influence of alcohol. I honestly didn't know if I was much of an articulate creative outside of the influence either.

Walking with a crutch made it easier, it didn't teach us how.

•••

• Page Twenty-Nine •

The easiest person to lie to was a loved one, they wanted to trust us the most. There were truly malicious and heartless people in the world, and they weren't the ones screaming "I hate you," they were the ones whispering "I love you." Still, I kept that between me and myself.

We didn't get to cry over the damage we caused, and think we were helping ourselves.

Options were presented, and I kept choosing the same stupid one. Rosa showed her true self repeatedly, and I repeatedly chose to involve myself with her. Who was I really mad at?

•••

• Page Thirty •

Kids didn't have a choice, and that was the most unfair part of life I saw. Perhaps contentment with trauma, as

part of humanity, would come to me when I was older and wiser. Or when I was prepared.

The experiences taking from us, left behind incomprehensible magic.

The anger I wanted to see past, wasn't see-through.

•••

• Page Thirty-One •

Marcus refused to discuss the root of his drinking problem, and like most roots, he let it extend down deep into the soil of his identity to create a hidden home. Both of his parents died in a car accident. Who held the authority to question his coping mechanism of choice? A coping mechanism felt like a cure, when its caress was warmth as we lay bare and shivering in darkness. It pulled us close, kissed us gently, and replaced the abrasive sandpaper of clarity, with a silk robe of temporarily

softened lines and rounded corners. Succumbing to its embrace, our senses were swayed into seeing the darkness as impossible to escape or understand.

Coping mechanisms, convinced us they were our sole means of survival or solace, in an unending cycle of anguish.

They functioned flawlessly that way. They lied.

•••

• Page Thirty-Two •

I was thinking about something my mother said, before we got off the phone, that sounded...off. She was turning fifty-nine in two months,and we were never closer, so I knew when something was wrong. I was a bartender sampling a cocktail through two skinny, black coffee straws, knowing there was an ingredient missing from the recipe.

Knowing who someone
was, meant knowing
when they were being
someone else.

●●●●●●

MERMAID DROWNING

We couldn't convince a mermaid they were drowning.

CHAPTER THREE

• Page Thirty-Seven •

My dad told me she was out there somewhere, comatose on the street with the rest of the dreamers. The City of Angels was more like the city of Atlantis: underwater, shark infested, lost. My dad's words. My mother bled ambition and didn't realize the consequences. The predators knew she was prey, and she knew less than she needed. My dad told me that. He said he was her life-jacket and tried to save her, but his rescue attempts felt more like kidnapping attempts.

The danger was real only once they realized for themselves; their sparkling aquamarine scales ensnared in desperation's jaws. By then, they were too far from the surface and too weak to fight their way back. One by one, the bubbles no longer floated upwards, and the water held its breath like an impassioned lover. Somewhere, submerged at a depth where sunlight was ancient myth, my mother was there, and hopefully still alive.

•••

• Page Thirty-Nine •

Her voice was soft, raspy, and each note felt like it told a little story of its own. Adopted, she was never on good terms with her parents, yet never told me why. The little tales told by the notes she sang never went away. Her voice was an image, reverberating off the walls in

my head, like the last gentle chime from a maturing music box. There was always a glaze of heartbreak, even when the song was a happy one.

Pain was hard to sing through, but when it was, tangible beauty reached out reluctantly. It's hand was outstretched for empathy, not synthesis.

The sentimentally protective sensation, inseparable from her song, was the most motherly thing I recalled about her.

•••

• Page Forty-One •

Watching him in that room, he was a necromancer, but the ghost he was attempting to contact was himself. I suppose, like most addicts, each drink was another shovel full of dirt thrown over memories he hoped to entomb. He didn't know that was useless. We couldn't drown or bury our sorrows, when air

didn't fill their lungs, regret did.

Memories didn't die, they waited.

•••

• Page Forty-Three •

The droughts in SoCal weren't only due to the forest fires. A different kind of thirst, dug through Angelenos one drop at a time. In a city where someone became the only thing everyone talked about every fifteen minutes, love and attention were pronounced almost identically. Hoses and lips were the tools used to extract sex, money, and adoration, passing it from one anxious enthusiast to another. The elemental mixture created more hunger, staining the teeth a dark red-orange.

Many of us chose to starve ourselves with what we ingested.

•••

• Page Forty-Six •

Skid Row was a homemade refugee camp. Both sides of the street were paneled with camping tents and wooden shacks, made from assorted pieces of graffitied and less-graffitied plywood. The sidewalk was clearly a front porch for the residents, so I walked on the street and watched for traffic. Nearly every structure was covered with the same blue tarps used for disaster relief, yet I saw no relief present. Portable outhouses with attached handwashing stations, were positioned near the larger clusters of tents, but the entire block smelled like one. I walked with my head and eyes down — as if they were weighted — and moved my feet to an imaginary treadmill spinning beneath them. Bass-heavy music played from a couple of the makeshift homes; laughter echoed off the asphalt. A barefooted man, wearing only a black garbage bag as short-shorts, hobbled passed me in the opposite direction on muddied feet darker than his attire. A woman sat on a rusty paint-bucket next to the curb, pouring water over her head from a shallow, plastic container to rinse soap from her hair into the gutter.

Was creativity accelerated by the death of comfort?

••••••

BEVERLY HILLS

CHAPTER FOUR

• Page Fifty-Seven •

Miracles took the most work. Too many didn't want work, only what work awarded. Regression was available in an array of makes and models. The mirror world was one of the more tangible delusions, it stared back at us the same way silence did. Was that why there were tales of vampires with no reflection? Did we need to invent creatures unable to see themselves backwards?

How did we find self, without first experiencing its loss?

What were we mad about? Vampires were interesting. They lived forever, never experiencing the loss of life, and consequently fed on life like Neapolitan ice cream sandwiches. Vampires represented those who hurt others, instead of finding a way to heal themselves. How could they see themselves as the source of harm without a reflection?

• • •

• Page Sixty •

Creatives sacrificed comfort for their creations, like tribal offerings to demanding deities. Experiences begged on bended-knee for interpretations from the observer. The risk attached to sharing our interpretations, was having them translated by the language of subjectivity. Artists volunteered themselves to be judged. The walk to the courtroom was on red carpet, and it wasn't red before they got there. Others didn't choose to be artists, they only chose to be. Artists used the broken pieces of themselves to build bridges. Others did other things. Art did not exist

outside of meaning.

Art was how artists were able to breathe.

•••

• Page Sixty-Three •

My attitude regarding how I treated people I didn't know, or didn't need, was growing easier to execute by the month. Disengage with disharmony.

If someone or something wasn't directly linked to the maintenance of my food, shelter, clothing, or means of acquiring such, they were not a necessity.

I was now okay with paying the price for being whoever I was, it felt refreshingly like being given free money.

•••

• Page Sixty-Six •

It was familiar. The whole scenario was familiar, so I was in a leup.**

** A leup (pronounced 'loop') is a life-cycle set in motion, by conscious or unconscious decisions, continually leading us back to the same people, places, and possessions. The individual choices creating a leup are often viewed as unrelated. Leups vary in intensity, often signaled by repeated deja vu, or the recognition of a repeated experience. For instance, a leup can be a cycle of making money, it can also be a cycle of choosing unfit romantic partners.

•••

• Page Seventy-Three •

Humans of all ages were still getting bullied because they enjoyed reading. That was still a thing. Were we surprised basic prejudices still plagued our perspectives? We were still mentally attacking each other for wanting to get smarter. Wasn't that a large part of the problem? And we said nothing—no one did—we just kept finding ways to be entertained enough to gouge out our eyes, but keep them at the same time. That was hardly an excuse.

When we surrounded ourselves with distractions, everything was.

We were what we allowed. What we allowed represented us directly.
As always.

• • •

• Page Eighty •

I remembered being where she was—not homeless—stuck deep and not knowing how to get out. The longer we were stuck, the further we drifted from the coastline of conscious existence. The return trip, from endlessly repeating a single sentence while limping through Beverly Hills on a Sunday, was a series

of layovers and connecting flights. Our energy shifted like Earth did. We did everything Earth did. We did what was done, we just did it in different environments. The homeless woman was a mirror, as we all were.

Honoring our conditioning over our calling, was the quickest way to lose ourselves.

• • • • • •

THOUGHTS DESCENDING

CHAPTER FIVE

• Page Eighty-Four •

Т he plummeting vehicle, was a purchase I made because I thought it would make me feel better. That was what we killed ourselves to make more, and more money for, right? So we could finally feel better than we did before, or at least better than someone else. I didn't feel any better, I felt worse.

Retail Therapy was real and one of my favorites. The things we owned didn't leave until we lost them.

Then I realized it was no different with people.

•••

• Page Eighty-Five •

Good and bad, were both words I wanted out of my vocabulary. Good and bad, were lazy ways to describe rewards and lessons. What we considered words to represent, defined much of our perspective.

Words defined our lives, yet we used them like we hated them.

Those words were either defined by ourselves or others; and those definitions informed, and gave direction to our decisions. The same happened earlier that evening. Passing by The Virgil, I thought of Virgil Abloh, knowing because of Virgil we knew there was a Virgil in all of us. The name Virgil was popularized by a Roman poet, but a poet of another medium redefined it. New definitions, new direction.

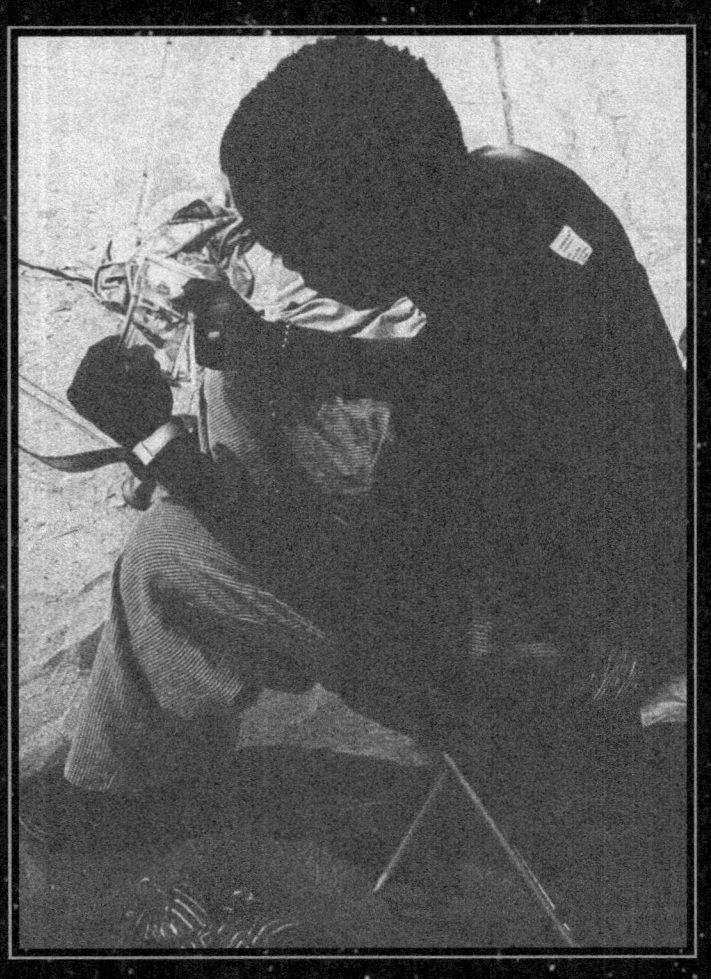

•••

• Page Eighty-Six •

Neither myself nor my two counterparts were notoriously tender, but we stayed up for hours doing coke and talking about everything we ran from. It felt like stopping, turning around, and finally facing off with the serial killer chasing you through the forest waving a machete — walking menacingly, as usual. The most sobering conversations, often happened when we were the opposite.

Some used drugs to silence the pain, others used them to feel the pain they silenced.

All three of us broke down emotionally, confessing our sins to one another like the good Catholics we never were.

•••

• Page Ninety-Two •

What struck me as stylized, was how the closer I was to dying, the slower everything went. I finally made a wrong turn I couldn't correct; I had time to think.

Slowing down was how we remembered, what we never wanted to forget.

Nothing worried me. I possessed nothing aside from the next few moments, realizing no other day was any different. Dying taught me a lot about living.

•••

• Page Ninety-Three •

The body only moved how the mind allowed.

The connections between the intersections of life required comprehension, or we would cut our umbilical cord while still in the womb.

The line between innovation and indolence, suffered from the occasional Purple Haze. The price of ignorance wasn't bliss, it was death.

• • •

• Page Ninety-Four •

When we meditated we could listen to our Unconscious. As we sat, if a thought arose we didn't consciously or willfully bring forward, we knew it was an unconscious one. Simple.

The Conscious and Unconscious mind were Yin and Yang, no different than our present and previous lives.

The parts of our minds we overlooked or avoided were on display. If we could see our Unconscious thoughts and emotions, swirling in front of us mentally, and how they didn't effect who we were presently, we saw how we chose to be altered by the stimuli we made contact with—voluntarily or involuntarily.

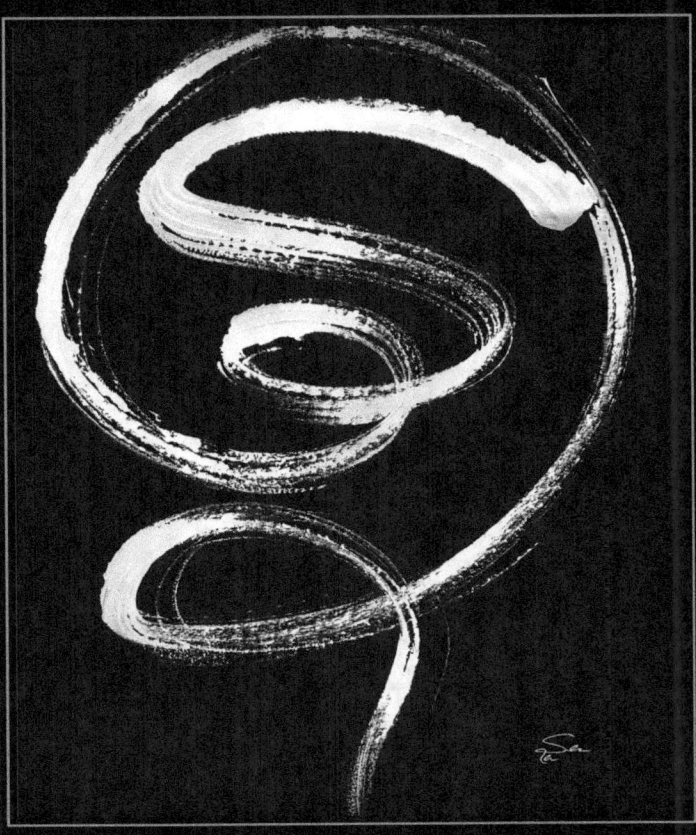

11 THOUGHTS

CHAPTER SIX

• Page Ninety-Nine •

When believing beasts to be beautiful was beneficial, we witnessed the confirmation of the anomalous. Miracles still came hard like women who were listened to, but I thanked every god they came at all. The miracles could decide they were needed elsewhere, in which case, I was excited for whomever shared their company.

Time passed, but certain aspects existed outside of it.

Los Angeles was a permanent residence of transcendence.

•••

• Page One Hundred & Three •

First the memories were like scratches on an old photograph, but soon the blemishes formed images of their own. Whatever was possible, was necessary.

Admitting ignorance initiated illumination.

It bothered me, the way we could have the knowledge of more than we put into practice. I was trying to practice more.

•••

• Page One Hundred & Eleven •

I preferred to set intentions and state what I wanted to gain, before taking anything with a psychoactive effect. Doing so, spoke to our Unconscious, partnering with it to activate areas of our minds —and the associated energy centers—our conditioning blocked. I used to party on psychedelics, now I prioritized and parasailed, through

unknown spaces of untold benefit. It was actually no different than saying grace before eating, or making a toast before drinking. We were telling our bodies and minds what to do, and how to feel, about the elements we were communing with.

Our experiences were easier directed, when focusing on the desired outcome and the reason behind it.

•••

• Page One Hundred & Fourteen •

Some wanted to be free, others wanted to be taken care of.

The consequences joining each decision were unique. Not good, not bad, just unique. When others did too much for us from too young an age, learning to do the same for ourselves was daunting. Those born into imbalanced homes, were given

a different ditch to dig their way out of, just like Arynn. Just like all of us. One flower grew in a meadow, another, on the corner of Pine Avenue and Market Street next to a streetlight.

•••

• Page One Hundred & Fifteen •

The power of wisdom, was the ability to realize our desired experience at will.

With wisdom, we desired harmony; shared interactions were of the highest. It was through wisdom, we could perform the alchemy of a life turned golden. We knew more and with more to navigate, but an easier time doing so. Eradicating fear through understanding, brought a level of ease. All was either a lesson, or reminder.

•••

• Page One Hundred &
Fifteen •

Walking, was our most
ancient and most personal
mode of transportation, and all
of us weren't able to do so.

The gift received by
fortunate children, was a
time to stroll the surface
of their mothers.

We did well to pay additional
honor, to the gifts we received
without request. Walking
taught us patience,
preparation, and how the
points we approached on our
journey could potentially alter
why we sojourned.

•••

• Page One Hundred &
Eighteen •

New bandages were placed on
top of the old, hoping to heal,
when they could only incubate
infection. It was no different
than the seasons.

The seasons of our lives,
repeated like the seasons
of the planet, if we did
nothing to change them.

No one was surprised, when
every year Spring came after
Winter. Yet, we were
surprised when generation
after generation experienced
the same wars, prejudices,
accomplishments, and dreams,
just on different scales.

•••••••

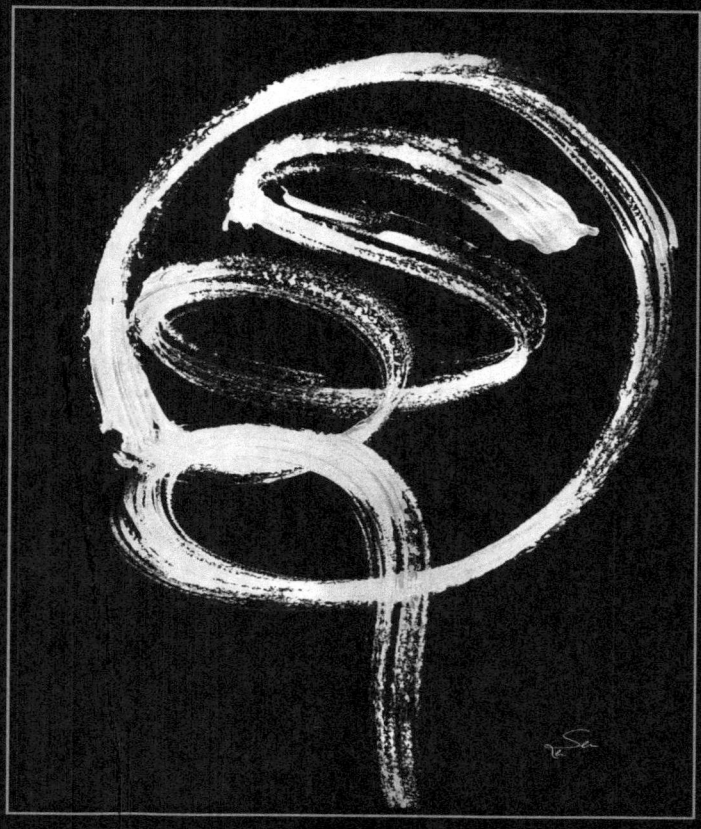

SAN FRAN

CHAPTER SEVEN

• Page One Hundred &
Twenty-Two •

More beauty than our brains could organize, surrounded us constantly, which I suspected was a source of collective agitation. Firmly misplaced anger was expressed, we couldn't locate a reason for; an emotion fostering frustration more than anything. Was our frustration developed from the countless available ways to enjoy our lives, and our limited capacity to undertake each captivating option?

Beauty also came in forms, we turned and looked away from.

• • •

• Page One Hundred &
Twenty-Three •

I heard it wise, to be weary of those who said they loved you before they knew you.

Those who loved in haste, often hated in the same fashion.

• • •

• Page One Hundred &
Twenty-Seven •

The desire to cradle the Unaware was, paternal. It was visible when parents were excused early from everywhere to handle child- related issues; when extra breaks were given to cigarette smokers, and budget additions made for added medical assistance for addicts. We were still a tribe. Helping those who were down, before knowing how they got there, became tradition, although the how mattered just as much as the why.

Over-assisting was the gentlest form of mutual sabotage.

•••

• Page One Hundred & Twenty-Nine •

Ignorance constructed confusion. Ignorance instituted entropy. I saw nothing there worthy to be desired, but that was subjective. I knew what I wanted, and what I ultimately needed those around me to want.

Escaped ignorance was sexy.

It was sexy seeking ways to decondition our minds. It was sexy seeking salubrious ways of developing, and maintaining, complementary relationships between mental, physical, and spiritual health. It was sexy living in choices decided freely, wisely, and in alignment.

•••

• Page One Hundred & Thirty •

The creation of processes to quickly complete necessary, yet unentertaining tasks, was how we kept the majority of our minds clear for pursuits of passion. Streamlining processes was supposed to keep us happier, not yolk us with brainless busy work. Foresight.

Overcompensation inconvenienced interpersonally, and the inconvenience led to conflict.

It was a recipe.

•••

• Page One Hundred & Thirty-Two •

Birthdays didn't matter much after we could drink and rent a car, but like a car, how we cared for ourselves internally, was externally telling. I still expected people older than I, to know something I didn't. We knew what we remembered. What we knew cared nothing of our age, only our competence. It was foolish inherently attaching time, to any kind of intelligence.

Immaturity enjoyed no excuse, nor did it have an age limit.

●●●

• Page One Hundred & Thirty-Three •

We felt bad, and did something to feel better before understanding there was nothing to feel bad about.

We carried too much carrying us backwards.

Our grip betrayed us when it held more than necessary.

●●●

• Page One Hundred & Thirty-Four •

Mayhem was exhilarating, and that's what some of us lived for, yet it would also be how we died. Limited time and space could be spent in, and around environments and personalities, before the experiences were part of us. There was only so long we could deny what made us feel alive.

Lying to ourselves was our leading cause of death.

●●●●●●

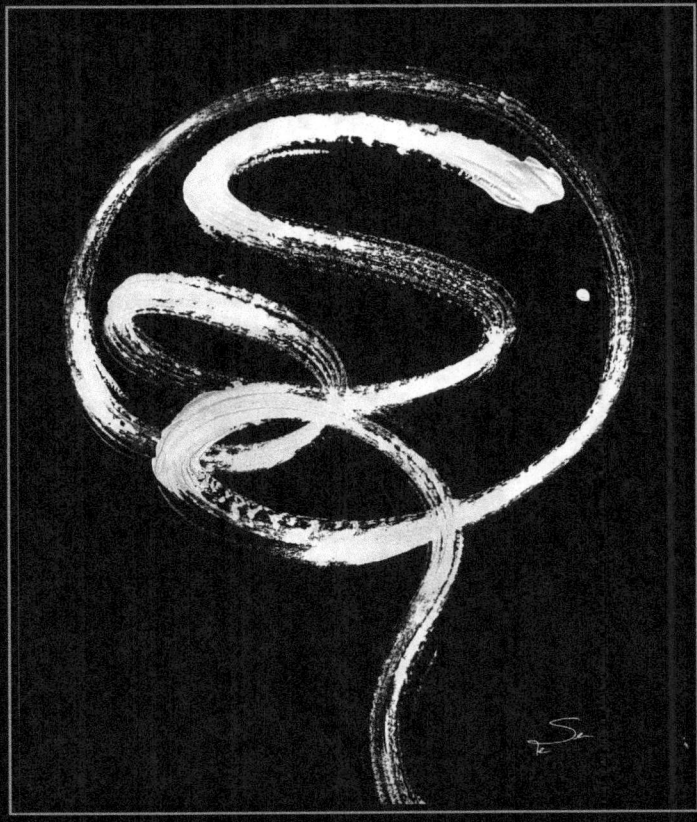

SAN BERNARDINO

CHAPTER EIGHT

• Page One Hundred &
Thirty-Eight •

Adults would fear the dark, as long as children were still given reason to.

Solitude was still the source of nightmares. If we couldn't sit silently without the TV on, or music, or a podcast, we could benefit by asking ourselves why. What was it we needed to confront? What did we not understand? What thoughts were we replacing with those of entertainers? What were we distracting ourselves from? Love could be a distraction. Planets were created in the vacuum of space, and by

extension, so were we. Stillness was where life began.

•••

• Page One Hundred &
Thirty-Nine •

The culinary arts were the most underrated, and the most tragic.

Chefs were the architects of flavorful fuel, designed for organic machinery.

Each piece was meant to inspire a desire, to devour it instantly and entirely. It was a love letter to our ego, French kissed into our taste buds. The culinary art form was appreciated by, the least number, for the shortest time. It was art designed for destruction.

•••

• Page One Hundred &
Forty •

There was a time for everything. Many enjoyed claiming time did not exist, or was an invention of humanity. The measurement of time, was simply the record of sequential events. Whether labeled "time" or something else, sequence gently enslaved us. The immortal reminders to prioritize and be patient, with persistence, were relentlessly and repeatedly written into creation. Remembering sugar was more addicting than cocaine, was key. All organic appearances were organically informative, while the inorganic additives deliberately deceived.

Part of the LA magic was nothing meant anything, so anything could mean everything.

•••

• Page One Hundred & Forty-Three •

They needed someone they could trust, even if they didn't know what it looked like personified, or how to respond to integrity. I needed someone who would allow me to be the parts of myself I buried, even if I didn't know how dark that was, or how to repay said privilege. Should those we interacted with need our help, or should they want it from recognizing its value? Was anything else really an equal exchange? Was the opposite not unhealthy?

Love and desperation didn't coincide.

•••

• Page One Hundred & Forty-Five •

Attempting to be right, for the sake of being right, only displayed the limit of our understanding. If doing so made us feel more complete, we could benefit by asking ourselves why. As long as we were satisfied with why we took a direction, and where it was going, why stop?

Engaging a new path began with reflecting on our past, our direct source for observing and studying the effects of our choices.

History wasn't bound to repeat itself, seasons were.

● ● ●

• Page One Hundred & Forty-Six •

A past we were still interpreting, was used to inform decisions on a future we couldn't predict.

I found our species surprisingly conceited, for one working with so little. I was practicing laughing at myself more, which wasn't easy for an adult who was picked on relentlessly as a child and adolescent. However, I was one of the clowns as well, like we all could be, I was just working on changing occupations.

MEDUSA SLAIN

CHAPTER NINE

• Page One Hundred &
Fifty •

I held my breath, shut my eyes, and listened. I was alone in the house now. The only sound in the kitchen was the low, droning hum rolling towards me from the tall, matte black refrigerator. I loved that sound. Something was deeply soothing about it, even now, like it was the heartbeat of the house, thumping steadily under my head as I lay on its chest.

How many of our desires
were fulfilled by
simplicity, once we
allowed them to be
fulfilled simply?

•••

• Page One Hundred &
Fifty-Two •

Opposites didn't attract,
complements did.

The Feng Shui was completed meticulously and purposefully, which was valuable since our mentality was affected by it. Our Unconscious Mind assumed, how we configured our external space represented our desire for the internal. The way energy moved through our homes, impacted our movement through life. The energy, was embodied by sensory stimuli speaking to us in unseen ways. The use of sounds, smells, colors textures, and shapes, contained benefits far deeper than selling merchandise and exposing toddlers to what their future held for them. The adult mind, even in its most jaded state, was still a sponge.

•••

• Page One Hundred &
Fifty-Four •

I thought what I made was really good, yet was told, like me, it was nothing special. I shouldn't have believed that but I did. As a shy, only child, who had trouble making friends and no cousins around the same age, the opinion of my parents was everything.

The world was mind.

Could we not see what parents were responsible for? Most of us had our branches, twisted into double double-helixes in their infancy. We did our best from there...

•••

• Page One Hundred &
Fifty-Five •

The creation was always the mirror, exposing the cracks in the creator.

When the creation did otherwise, were those not anomalies? The anomaly was part of the pattern, it didn't represent the pattern in its entirety. Genius represented universally dispersed potential, not the potential all would unlock. As cliché as it was, it all started at home. Every aspect of life was a story. Whether the stories were what we told ourselves, or what others told us, they shaped and reshaped our value of life and our place within. It didn't matter if the stories were real or not.

•••

• Page One Hundred &
Fifty-Seven •

There was no such thing as being a better person, we only became more or less of who we chose to be.

I didn't know if I was becoming more or less of me, and gave up on trying to figure it out. The rules we placed on ourselves, and pretended we agreed with blindly following, were brainless. We were born into, or gave birth to, families of strangers we grew to familiarize ourselves with over time. These people weren't chosen. Our parents, children, siblings, aunts, uncles, were all forced onto us. Even if we chose to make a child, it was still culturally looked down upon to simply give them away if we were unhappy with our dynamic. Adoption was obviously a thing, but still. Kids were made without permission, so we didn't get to wash our hands of them without leaving a permanent residue.

•••

• Page One Hundred & Sixty •

Our divinity was hidden when our essence was. The eye of the beholder held beauty, and at times, it was held away from the beautiful. When did the most desirable path, become the road most trampled?

Who taught us rarity wasn't the only thing we shared?

Who taught us to hate what we were? Who taught us to live lesser?

••••••

ALIGNED

CHAPTER TEN

• Page One Hundred &
Sixty-Two •

Those living on the street, made choices at breakfast most wouldn't survive by lunch. Their raw appearance, was a reminder of reality's artistic indifference regarding medium or material. Obvious inspiration abounded, and those with access were taking notes quicker than bank thieves. The layers, the oversizing, the rips, the holes, the paint—down to the palette—were hardly reimagined in the creation of bubblegum, affluent-only, hyper-capitalist-approved versions of the organic. Pastels and bleach stains symbolized faded vibrance, from living unsheltered for upwards of twenty-four hours per day. Rays of California sun painted on whatever was worn, the same as California painters. The colors weren't style choices, they were battle scars.

If those beneath the stars looked up for inspiration, perhaps the stars looked down for theirs.

• • •

• Page One Hundred &
Sixty-Six •

The processes growing and building us collectively, broke and rebuilt us individually.

Too many told us we were awarded for avoidance. Where we learned, and where we practiced what we learned, were separate. Barricades weren't always blockages.

• • •

• Page One Hundred &
Sixty-Nine •

A myriad of paths and purposes, presented themselves once we prepared. Preparation was a personal process for each of us.

Altering our path for those still preparing, erased our progress.

The more progress preserved, the more progress perpetuated.

•••

• Page One Hundred &
Seventy •

There were times we regressed, in order to relearn. Meditating and working with energy, worked so well for me I thought I outgrew it.

Our lungs didn't outgrow oxygen.

I was almost back to the point, where what others thought of what worked for me changed nothing. Why would adults argue over opinions?

•••

• Page One Hundred &
Seventy-One •

Energy moved when it was refocused.

Stopping the flow of energy was never an option at our disposal. Energy couldn't be destroyed, what made us think it could be halted? When energy was refocused there was change, so refocus was how we changed cycles. Only the past was absolute. The future and present evolved simultaneously.

•••

• Page One Hundred &
Seventy-Five •

Wisdom was the outcome of choosing to examine the patterns in our experience, then creating an avenue to comprehend them thoroughly.

Only once we pursued wisdom, did we have anything worth saying; and only once we were asked was it said. I needed someone who knew enough, to know the value they brought to an interaction, while knowing everything around us imparted everything needed.

•••

• Page One Hundred & Eighty •

Ascension, was the cyclical journey of walking deeper in our divinity. The journey took longer for many of us, because we chose to act out of alignment to satisfy requests from the ego. The ego wasn't bad or wrong. The ego thought of the present only, and of itself only. Without the ego we would be dead. The ego, yelled to save ourselves because it was too valuable to die, and by extension, so were we. Without the ego, we also lived in unending contentment. I would ponder the parallel perspectives later; the philosophy could wait.

A fear of loss, was a fear of gain.

••••••

11 LIGN

CHAPTER ELEVEN

Good and evil were one hundred percent subjective, meaning the power associated with them was the same.

•••

• Page One Hundred & Eighty-Nine •

Knowledge was a form of energy. Energy required a framework to be utilized for any formulation. Energy existing outside of a measurable framework was immeasurable, unidirectional, and without a perceivable pattern. For thousands of years the words karma, sin, and crime, globally agreed on unclear, speculative definitions. Karma described perceived accountability, which was interesting because proximity mattered. Holding hands with the guilty, held us to sharing their fate. Our karma may be a car accident, in which case we should drive alone. Stifling our perspective wouldn't expand it.

• Page Two Hundred & Two •

I was working on representing who I was more accurately, especially in public. What opportunity required us to rush?

When we were ready, it was time, and it would not be time until we were ready.

Our only responsibility, was continuing the forward momentum of pursuing purpose and understanding, like walking confidently towards one who awaited us.

•••

• Page Two Hundred &
Three •

How sympathy and empathy
were expressed, said nothing
about where it was directed,
and everything about the
director.

Being fake, defeated the
purpose of being alive.

The purpose of being alive, of
course, being to do whatever
we wanted. The grander
purpose of being alive was
finding how we could help.
Help was what we would all
need.

•••

• Page Two Hundred &
Four •

We ingested spirits of varying
magnitudes into our bodies
daily. Wasn't "spirit" another
term for a form of energy?
Did possessions historically
occur in more rural areas, due to
the energy being more available
with less obstruction? Drug
addicts, and those with severe
mental illness, were said to often
display the same symptoms as
the spiritually possessed. Was
that considered coincidence?

The scientific and
spiritual explained the
same concepts, in ways
differing perspectives
could comprehend.

•••

• Page Two Hundred &
Seven •

The ability to ask the question,
separated the human from the
hamster. Bold inquiry returned
bold insight. Why did we die?
Because we lived. Dying a
death where we honored
ourselves, instead of our
conditioning, only made us
wiser and further aligned. The
further into alignment we
moved, the less we acted or
lived in ignorance.

The pain we caused, only
produced more of the
pain we aimed to avoid.

Ignorance closed our eyes to
the obvious.

• • •

• Page Two Hundred &
Ten •

What did Satan mean?
Obstacle. Many of us based
most of our lives on what was
good or evil, right or wrong.
The embodiment of evil was
an obstacle.

Obstruction was a voice
in our minds, praising the
power of instant
gratification without
mentioning the slow
regression.

Only after indulging the
obstructive did we see how far
back it moved us, and how
much work was necessary to
return to where we were.

• • • • • •

SAINT MOE

CHAPTER TWELVE

• Page Two Hundred &
Fifteen •

I was no where close to buying a gourmet pizza, let alone a house. I wanted his son's success to be motivating, however, it was easy to feel like I would never catch up. But who was I chasing? The owners of the lives we coveted, didn't know we existed and didn't need to. I wasn't chasing Moe's kid.

Was the goal getting what we wanted, or getting what others did that we didn't?

The hardest thoughts for me to navigate were those of comparison, the variables involved were never forthcoming.

•••

• Page Two Hundred &
Seventeen •

Not being where we wanted, didn't mean we weren't closer.

You know? But, we had to try different ways of getting things done to figure the things out. We discover ourselves by interacting with new environments and people, and taking note of the current ones.

•••

• Page Two Hundred &
Twenty-One •

Being ourselves was the easiest path to choose, although not the easiest to see through til the end.

Loving ourselves meant doing what we loved, even if we were the only ones who loved what we did. Love could mean

being by ourselves, sometimes for a long time, but that was when we explored who we were without interruption or influence.

•••

• Page Two Hundred & Twenty-Six •

War is a form of communication.

It should obviously be the very last one we throw on the table, however, it exists now because it's still needed. War speaks to our animal, not our intellect. It was one of our options we kept around because, like in all conflict, winning feels good. And sometimes losing does too. War was one of the languages of the lower chakras, like Philosophy was of the higher. It's what you guys are calling your higher and lower-selves or vibrations, now. The higher understands the concept of an experience, while the lower understands its texture.

•••

• Page Two Hundred & Twenty-Nine •

Multitasking deviates our focus, and is either a symptom of greed or poor planning.

We're already running on the fumes of a long lost attention span. I'm trying to keep the little I have left.

•••

• Page Two Hundred & Thirty-Four •

The entertainment experiences only understood once felt, were most coveted, yet the lessons taught that way shook us loose from lethargy without a window of warning.

The purpose of life was growth, as it did so without direction.

Just like dying. I thought of
that every time I saw a flower
bend towards the sun.

•••

• Page Two Hundred &
Forty-Five •

We can get what we ask for—
and we usually do—yet our
expectation of how our
answered request will appear,
causes the hand reaching for
the other to miss.

We have to say what we
mean, if we want what
we say to happen.

Do we want to move
somewhere new for the
scenery, or are we moving to
find ourselves? To start a new
life? To find inspiration?
Clarity, was of more benefit
than caution.

••••••

BEVERLY'S HILL

CHAPTER THIRTEEN

My ankle really hurt.

Bad.

I wanted to stop walking, but I didn't have time to waste.

Thinking rest would slow us down, was like thinking food would make us hungrier.

I blamed my hunger for why I couldn't think straight.

I was hungry, and I knew if Lydia didn't have anything she could share, Alfredo would.

I didn't know Alfredo long, yet he was one of the kindest, and quietly wise people I knew.

When I first met him, he said his name was Alfredo, like the sauce, and he was both the sauce and the seasoning.

Lydia said she was Lydia, like the saint, and she was a saint just like I imagined the other one was.

I didn't know much about dead saints.

I thought as little about dead people as possible; it was challenging enough being present with the living ones.

I couldn't wait to put these bags down; I didn't know how many I carried—I needed to recount.

Life was heavier than I wanted it to be.

I felt like I was walking with Moses across the desert; I didn't know when I would get to my Promised Land either.

The night was nice though; a plane flew overhead, low enough for me to read the airline name; an attractive couple dressed for date night, argued under a glowing full moon.

I hated hearing people argue.

The yelling was an odd counterpart to the song playing from the wine bar half a block in front of me—'S Wonderful by Joao Gilberto.

I wanted to get as far away from the couple as I could, in the shortest amount of time, but not with this stupid ankle.

My whole right leg was pretty bad, if I was being honest with myself.

Being honest with myself wasn't my favorite, I liked

hearing what I liked to hear—if I was being honest.

Everyone asked for honesty, yet there were only more questions once it arrived.

People had everything to say, yet nothing to do.

My motto was simple: make shit easy or leave.

I was limping down some god…blessed street in Beverly Hills some where, yet it felt like moving backwards through a dream.

If the couple arguing outside the bar saw me getting closer, they were hiding it better than the emotions we couldn't face.

Something in my left shoe aggressively rubbed into the right side of my achilles—a rock or something.

I kept wiggling my foot around back and forth between steps, which wasn't helping and only raised my annoyance vertically.

The weight of my bags, made them swing like broken suspension-bridges when I moved; I was really just trying not to fall on my face.

Again.

The guy cursed at the girl; she cursed back louder and emphasized with her hands.

The energy we used in battle could instead be used in love.

Love was another word for alignment.

I didn't think the couple knew what I knew, and I wanted to tell them, but…I unfortunately—that just wasn't the person I was.

We all lived amongst the stars, yet it was easy to forget that made us one of them.

Without practicing discernment, we only saw what wasn't.

We were all falling, we might as well fall in love.

What would happen if we treated each other like we were in love with one another?

What else did we have time for?

It wasn't like I was the only one dying, everyone was.

We were all dying everyday.

My last boyfriend passing-away, taught me a lot about living.

I believed we missed those we loved before we met them.

When I met Logos at Lynn's funeral, he had nine weeks to live.

Harmonically, the loss of one life, allowed us both to create a new one we shared together.

Something told me life always worked that way, and always would.

We dated, and it was the greatest relationship of my life.

I thought the intensity of the experience was specific to him and his circumstances; I thought our love was richer because he was dying.

Was it the knowledge of our limited time together, making every second taste like the first time he played my heartbeat from the inside?

I forgot all of our time here was shockingly short.

Love was a fragment we treated like forever, yet it departed as it arrived.

We were spoiled with the sweetest moments, while seated with the clearest view.

Everyone we met was a fading miracle.

What did the terminally ill have time to debate?

I looked in the mirror, and saw someone handcuffed to caution.

We were dying uncertain and unappreciative.

Our path would be driven more carefully and, graciously, if we remembered we lost value once we left the lot.

We couldn't trade-in bodies like leased cars—not yet; not publicly.

That was why a skull was my first and favorite tattoo.

My second one said, "5150", and I wore it with the pride of a Purple Heart medal, like everyone else who chose to brand themselves.

The iconography of the skull was to remind us daily we were dying, no matter how shiny the paint was.

A reminder of our mortality was a reminder of the miraculous.

If death was like falling asleep and never waking up, sleeping was like resurrecting from the dead.

Waking up was a mathematical miracle.

I could have easily stayed dead; the planet didn't need more participants.

People went to sleep nightly, not knowing their tossing and turning was being turned off indefinitely.

We were all falling, we could be nicer to those we passed on the way down.

The skull and bones, represented more than pirates and clandestine organizations.

The arguing couple either forgot what mattered, or was never introduced.

The words we wasted made death sentences swifter.

The illusion of ownership wasn't always fatal, yet it was always a thief.

Unnecessary anger stole time from us all.

Was stealing time, the same as stealing life?

I hoped I stole no time from anyone I aligned with.

Concepts, events, and people, in mysterious alignment, were often mislabeled as ironic.

I used to think it was irony connecting the distant and disregarded to one another.

Irony was another way to say, misunderstood harmony.

Irony was a myth.

The ironic was harmonic — harmony realized.

My observation of harmony revealed the *syrc* (s-urk) swirled myself into, like the markings on seashells.

A syrc was a ring of repeated interactions, entered voluntarily or involuntarily when equilibrium was chosen over evolution.

Some still called it a leup, however, it was clearer to have different words for different experiences.

A nice woman I didn't know who spoke to me earlier and gave me five dollars, called the phenomenon a syrc; her name was Carmen.

I asked her if she was a *corentice,* and she said yes.

The knowledge of the *corentice* was extensive, so I called the phenomenon what she did.

I had a feeling she was one of them; the guy with her was cute, although clearly not as elevated — probably why they were together.

The Carmen lady shuffled two tumbled stones in her right hand, each flat on two sides — magnetite, naturally magnetic.

Apologizing, her fingers stopped moving the objects which clicked when connected; I said it was fine and asked why she had them.

Organic magnetism was magic to her, and the reflective charcoal surface of the stone shared a subtle symbolism.

The darkest aspects of existence were reflections like all others, tools used to see the sides of ourselves others usually saw first.

Magnets reminded us, that what was intrinsically aligned would effortlessly attract.
Positive and negative were irrelevant.
Interacting with organically magnetized elements, was said to be interacting with a looped echo of Earth's magnetic field.
Shuffling magnetite was a focused-meditation, aimed at reducing perceived inner polarity, increasing more efficient direction of physical and metaphysical magnetism.
Carmen unstacked the top stone, released it, and it snapped instantly into its near identical pair.
Things fell into place once we let go, as long as we let go when pulled to.
The sight of separation was shortsighted.

We were the only one alive.
Together.

The arguing couple on the sidewalk subsided slightly — once I was a few feet away — and the man stood behind the woman with his hands securely on her shoulders.
She still looked very angry.
I would take a man's hands on my shoulders, over the pinching, plastic shopping bags, and my happiness would be evident and audible.
Joao Gilberto was less audible also, as the last violin notes of the song bowed their heads and their bows in unison.
The street wasn't as rowdy as usual, and the added silence from the couple accentuated the cries from the bags I carried, and limps I dragged to carry them.
The distractions were gone, and I immediately wanted them returned; the fingers of my mind impatiently rummaged for a new toy.
Shifting our focus to the problems of others, made ours seem smaller, yet only momentarily.

Adjusting our minds changed our perception of reality, not it's presentation.

I lived most of my life in my head, like most did, however, unlike most, I knew I did and didn't deny it.

While walking, I could feel my lips moving and the vibration of words being said.

I wasn't consciously doing anything, I was just too tired to stop what was in progress.

My mouth was saying something about, not liking where I was, or not expecting things to be like they were—I was trying not to listen.

Finally, I passed the couple, out of range of their eyes pressing against me like the pressure to surpass societal milestones.

I didn't react to their gawking, and I could still feel my mouth moving on its own, and my ankle throbbing like a subwoofer.

Their opinion of me didn't matter, I only somewhat maintained one of myself.

The thing where I spoke involuntarily, was my *aconscious mind* replacing the functions of my conscious one.

The aconscious mind, or aconscious, was short for auto-conscious (auto, referring to, autonomic), a more accurate description for what was called the unconscious or subconscious mind.

The aconscious described the part of our minds pumping blood through our bodies, as well as where our intuitive insight and trauma was stored.

It functioned with, or without, conscious direction, yet always automatically, internalizing and interpreting stimuli.

Because of a few regressive decisions I made, and a few others made for me, I struggled to balance my brain.

I usually let it win and do the talking, that way I could at least have time to think in peace.

Unchecked aconscious expression was yelling, multiple one-sided conversations, disjointed sentences, ideas, and actions.

While we slept, our unregulated cognitive classroom was uninterrupted.

Dreams and delusions originated from the same part of the mind, one displayed what was in front of us, the other what wasn't.

Our Aconscious spoke an ageless language of images, emotions, and experiences.

How was dream interpretation different from interpreting any other part of our lives?

Wasn't the symbolism we interacted with, all internally digested with similar mental procedures?

Dreams were part of reality because we were alive while dreaming, yet we categorized them as somehow singular.

Weren't dream interpreters just life coaches, analyzing the one-third of our lives we spent asleep?

I understood how some things worked, and I was really pretty smart, just not in the ways I needed.

Not everything making sense, made a noticeable difference.

At the next light I would make a left to cross the street, and then keep going straight until after the liquor store, where the chain-link fence around back was busted open.

If Alfredo wasn't there, Lydia definitely would be: the cave dweller who could create a cave anywhere out of anything. Her tent was big enough for both of us, and she managed magically not to get it stolen, mostly because of how seldom she left it alone.

Alfredo's ex burned his last tent down to the zippers a couple months ago, but that same week, someone in Venice gave him the thickest sleeping bag I'd ever seen.

Nothing was taken from us.

He let me try it, and I was speechless once I got inside — and sweating.

I was also speechless last night, after me and Lydia stumbled into a four-hour-series of serious conversation topics, while Alfredo was passed out holding half of a hamburger.

Lydia and Alfredo were both obviously healthier, younger, and more youthful than I was, so the openness and introspection from her was unexpected.

I basically met her right before Alfredo lost his tent.

We started off just talking about our favorite musicians and albums, and she shared an unusual angle about music and sound.

Lydia said our bodies were used to house, interpret, and transmit energy.

Dancing was how frequency and vibration moved the body.

We didn't move to music, we were moved by it.

She said she wanted to be a musician in a past life, that was why she moved to California.

LA was America's North Star for artists, aliens, and addicts.

I couldn't consistently tell the difference between them, and didn't know if there were any differences worth noting.

Last night was when Lydia told me she was an addict, and if she didn't say anything, I would never have guessed—it didn't show at all.

She said, having something masked holding us back wasn't always best.

The hidden problems, also hid from the solutions.

When we saw people for who we understood them to be internally, externally they appeared the same.

Lydia sounded like a professor; I only knew a little about how addiction worked chemically.

We became dependent on the elements and environments we overexposed ourselves to, without healthy periods of separation.

It was an equation.

Lydia turned the music down after I said that, and thought for a second.

I was laying on my back next to her in her tent, looking up at the night sky through the skylight.

Lydia was laying down also but sat up, folded her legs, and cracked her neck on each side.

She said there was another side of addiction she didn't hear brought up as much as needed.

Most addicts didn't know what else to do.

They weren't told, they weren't taught, and by the time they were, they were so attached to the addiction, that removing it from their diet was like removing water from soil.

A raised level of understanding, allowed us to escape with an energy of discovery instead of desperation.

Many addicts suffered spiritually or psychologically from *hyperpresence*.

Hyperpresence was forgetting we were not always where we were, or who we were, nor would we be.

The hyperpresent were often indifferent towards future-planning, as the utility of the present was understood and prioritized solely.
If we were taught life was inherently painful, why wouldn't any way of soothing that pain seem sensible?
Pain was another word for attachment.
I incorrectly assumed Lydia was addicted to some drug, survival was her dependency.
She was raised having to survive, and that became a comfortable default setting she didn't know could switch off.
Extended periods of stability and safety made her unbearably anxious.
I didn't know security could feel like strangulation.
She said her last boyfriend almost killed her, just like the previous one, yet she knew consciously distancing herself from them was a must.
The temptation dragging her backwards by the ankles wouldn't be doing so against her will.
We could save ourselves from anything we were honest about.
Self-awareness wasn't celebrated enough.
Clarifying our comprehension of the concepts taught to us, clarified the concepts we discovered.
Lydia saw the syrc she sat in as clearly as she saw the Sun in clear skies.

Clarity wasn't contagious, however, it could be contracted like any other infection.

I was ready to see what she saw for myself, and I couldn't wait to lay next to her again and find out more.
When I met Lydia and Alfredo I told them my name was Beverly, like the Hills, and soon I would be over mine…in one way or another.

GLOSSARY

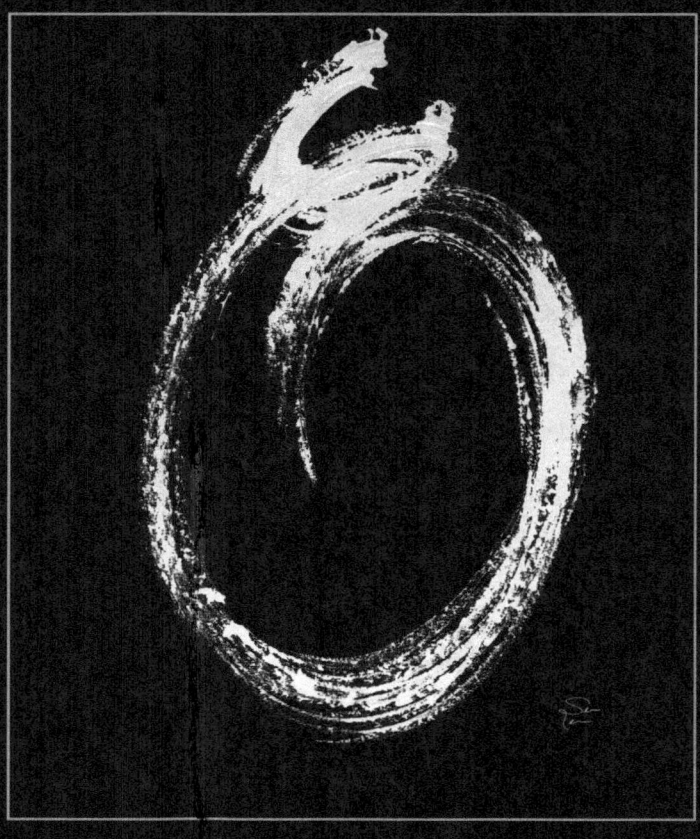

STABILIZATION
ASSIMILATION LAW

Some are pulled to question every action and thought, regarding what it means to be alive, dead, or otherwise.

A recognition is made, of a personal disconnect to traditionally conditioned perspectives.

The most elementary interpersonal, personal, and cultural sensibilities of our species, are interacted with and observed, with pronounced objectivity.
The daily maintenance of mental stability, is then achieved by exercising a level of adherence to standardized practices.

Was the responsibility of those questioning the current societal customs and compliances, knowing when and how to do so?

Nothing overlooked.

Statement: inquiry.

Implores:

The Frailty of Hate: hatred arises from unexamined and unresolved traumatic experiences, increasing and perpetuating patterns producing undesired experiences.

Do we choose hatred, while also understanding its origin and outcome?

GENERAL OWNERSHIP PHENOMENON

Possession is an illusion.

We own nothing.
We keep nothing.
We lose nothing.
We are free.

From the items we purchase, create, and collect, to the people we befriend, give birth to, and love, none are exempt.
The illusion of ownership, is revealed to be one of the most destructive devices used to validate humanity's existence.
The promise and expectation of permanence, is either introduced through deception, ignorance, or irrationality.

Everything is borrowed.

Statement: detachment.

Implores:

The Release Reception: when finding ourselves without an interaction or item—we enjoy having in our lives, and desire that it return—embracing that it is also perfect where it is, and remembering it was borrowed to begin with, crates the necessary space for reconnection and rediscovery.

If we feel unprepared to let something go, are we truly prepared to let it in?

AUTHORIST FUTURISM

An alignment with the determination, that present action shifts events of an undecided future, unlocking possibilities which would otherwise go undiscovered.

Authorists push forward, plotting ways to direct the directionless, viewing their influence as practical and progressive.

Authorist Futurism encapsulates vision, invention, and firmness.

Statement: production.

Implores:

The Journey of Genesis: paths of the deepest passion, purpose, and alignment, are discovered by first pursuing current personal progressive paradigms.
The path we plan to take, reveals the path we love.

No direction is arbitrary.

Creating the current behind our course.

SURRENDERIST FUTURISM

An alignment with the determination, that present action is part of what has previously been set in motion, with all possibilities organically presenting themselves.

Surrenderists let go, attracting ways to maneuver harmoniously with their environment, viewing their influence as impractical and unnecessary.

Following the current, rather than creating it.

Surrenderist Futurism encapsulates fluidity, reception, and communion.

Statement: patience.

DISPLEASING DECISION CONSOLATION

A ltering our view, in order to enjoy the undesired or the inalterable.

Displeasing Decision Consolation, is the process of shifting our interpretation of an undesirable decision, or the characteristics of a selection, by distorting our perception so circumstances translate more favorably emotionally.

We tell ourselves a story, producing an appreciation of what we don't want or don't value, decreasing the possibility of further dissatisfaction and disappointment.

Settling for the sake of ease.
Settling happily.

Softer sight.

Statement: acceptance.

BASE BARTER PRINCIPLE

All interactions include an energetic exchange, tangible or intangible.

Even generosity is traded for gratitude.
Time and energy are traded perpetually.

Although the transference may go undetected by one, or all involved, and what is transferred may not be directly proportional, it exists and transpires nevertheless.

Mutual equal gain.

Statement: worth.

Implores:

Adversity Indication: when experiencing personal difficulty, this is the act of choosing to openly express or display it — calling out for help. This signals our immediate surroundings, and its inhabitants, that assistance is required for part of the interconnected whole.
Adversity Indication is also initiated, when we deplete ourselves physically or energetically — giving all we have — shifting us into a more favorable position to receive additional external support.

If we have yet to explore the value of vulnerability, how can we understand the power of vulnerability?

EMOTIONAL TRUTH THEORY

A version of truth exists, which is true only in the moment it is experienced or expressed.

It is always changing, as is characteristic of emotions themselves.

The associated words, actions, and thoughts are genuine when generated, however, their level of validity fluctuates with time, interpretation, and desire.

All within reason.

Statement: logic.

FALSEHOOD THEORY

L ies and truths, are each stories we choose to accept or
reject.

Contrasting narratives are tools, teaching what the other will
not.

Recognizing the individual effects, does each have an
interaction where one is more progressive than the other?

What is considered as fact, further develops with
understanding, as is what is confirmed as such.

The truth allows for a balanced decision to be made, a lie
allows the opposite.
Is balance always the desired outcome?

Polarized purpose.

Statement: utility.

THE CATALYTIC PRINCIPLE

R ight and wrong are opinions, there are only catalysts and inhibitors.

A being, act, or event, either encourages transformation (catalyst) or reinforces the habitual (inhibitor).

Evolution or revolution.

Whether catalysts or inhibitors are considered positive or negative, is a perspective of our own invention, used to compartmentalize functionality rather than comprehend it.

Statement: harmony.

I mplores:

Compasis—also known as, the Necessity of All.
Each step taken in time, being taken by everything in existence at once.
None happens without all.
What exists is needed.
What is needed exists.
What is experienced is allowed.

Where is imperfection found?

AEONILISM

Aeonilism is a perpetually expanding interpretation of expressed universal interconnection.
A philosophy bringing calm and cohesion to the mind, through 9 Observations allowing us dissolve instilled opposition, and bridge parallel perspectives.

Discovery, understanding, and evolution as a way of life; striving to ascend past acts of ignorance and misguidance.
All is done to further all.
None is devalued to confirm the value of another.
Divinity is defined in many ways all describing the same.
As Always.

CLARIF

Clarifs recognize the authentic nature of people and places, and reveal this recognition without bias. Some do so unintentionally, others deliberately, yet all do so purposefully.

CORENTEA

Corentea (ko-ren-tay) studied the patterned flow of energy within a given medium—the current—understanding how the energy's character shifted with the framework. Energy was directionless on its own, the medium provided the possibility of direction. Corentea was seen as a *Surrenderist* approach, experiencing and interpreting the currents of energy more than manipulating their motion.

The *corentice* (ko-ren-tis) were the students, eternally learning.

• additional expressions and concepts from the world of LA on LSD and more—
visit aeonaes.com •

° THE SCRIBE °

Sean Aeon is an author, artist, philosopher, and the sole-creator behind a unique intersection of illuminating material incorporating literature, philosophy, and visual art.

His body of work supports and inspires self-exploration, self-awareness, and deeper understanding, through philosophical, psychological, and spiritual commentary.

The examination of universal, inherent, and evident interconnectivity, is central in his fictional narratives, demonstrated through mindful storytelling.
Sean's writing style is a combination of James Baldwin, Alan Watts, Frank Miller, and Alan Moore.

Books by Sean Aeon:
Written By Chameleons: Tales of Hollywood Wake-Ups
Written By Silence: Tales From the Divine
LA on LSD
The Outsider's Mind: A Collection of Short Stories & Quotes
Fairytales From Within

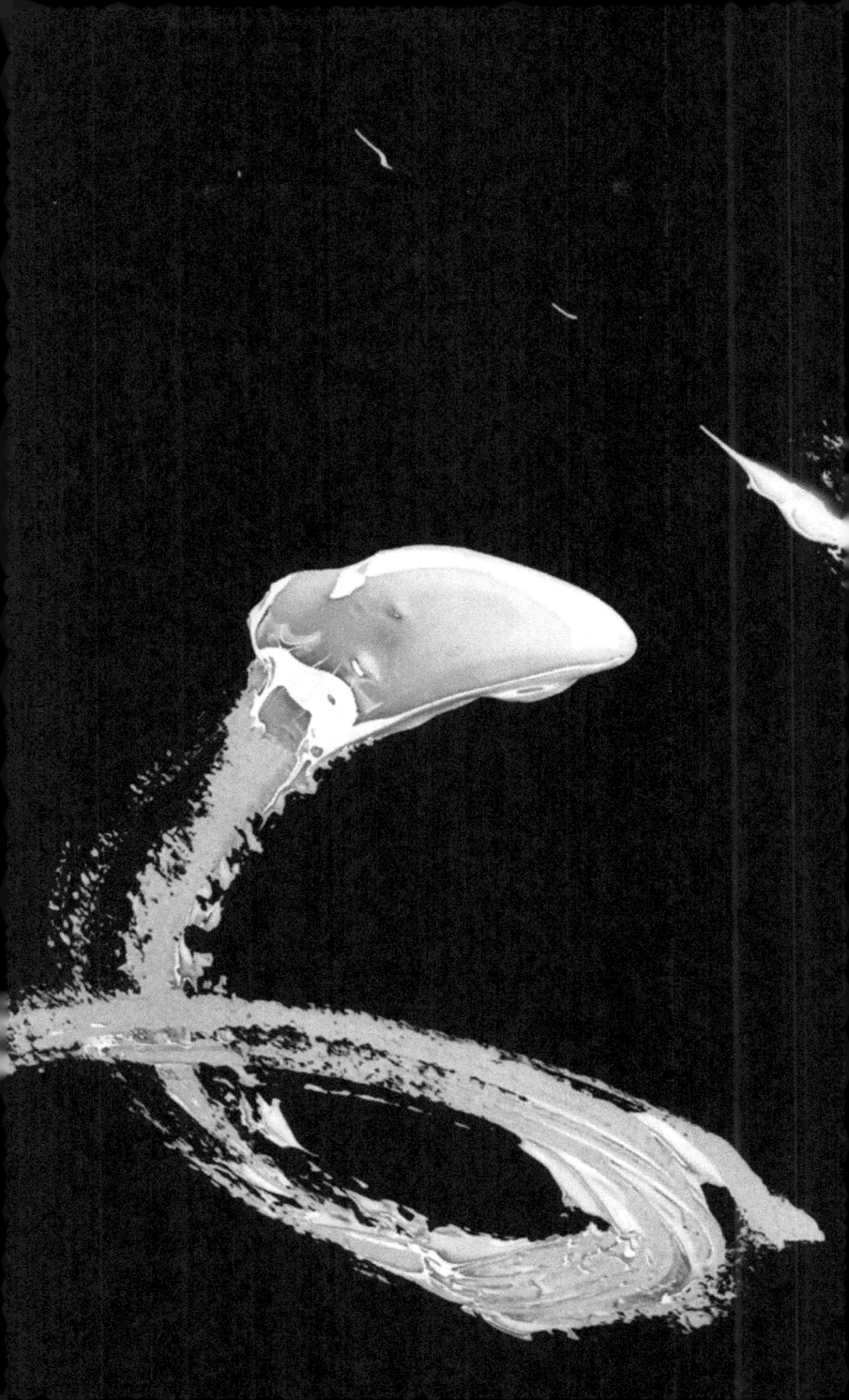

www.ingramcontent.com/pod-product-compliance
Lightning Source LLC
Chambersburg PA
CBHW060651260626
47161CB00008B/3088